PUFFIN BOOKS

MAD MYTHS: MUST FLY!

Steve Barlow was born in Crewe. He has been a refuse collector, laundry-van driver, postal worker and puppeteer. He spent four years teaching English in a village school in Botswana, where a valid excuse for not having your homework was: 'A goat ate it, sir!'

He currently teaches performing arts at a college in Nottingham. He lives in Derbyshire with his wife, two children and a cat called Captain Birdseye. He enjoys sailing, walking, listening to music and shouting at politicians on the telly.

Steve Skidmore was born in Birstall in Leicestershire. He has never been to Crewe. He is younger and much shorter than Steve Barlow. The first fact annoys Barlow, but Skidmore doesn't go on about it because of the second.

He has had a variety of jobs, including one that involved counting pastry lids on meat pies. He has not eaten a meat pie since. He enjoys most sports, especially Rugby Union, and supports Leicester Tigers.

Steve Barlow and Steve Skidmore have written quite a few books together, including the *Mad Myths* series.

Other books by Steve Barlow and Steve Skidmore

MAD MYTHS: STONE ME!
MAD MYTHS: MIND THE DOOR!
MAD MYTHS: A TOUCH OF WIND!

VERNON BRIGHT AND FRANKENSTEIN'S
HAMSTER
VERNON BRIGHT AND THE MAGNETIC BANANA

SURFERS

Mad Myths

MUST
FLY!

Steve Barlow & Steve Skidmore

Illustrated by
Tony Ross

PUFFIN BOOKS

PUFFIN BOOKS

Published by the Penguin Group
Penguin Books Ltd, 27 Wrights Lane, London W8 5TZ, England
Penguin Putnam Inc., 375 Hudson Street, New York, New York 10014, USA
Penguin Books Australia Ltd, Ringwood, Victoria, Australia
Penguin Books Canada Ltd, 10 Alcorn Avenue, Toronto, Ontario, Canada M4V 3B2
Penguin Books India (P) Ltd, 11 Community Centre, Panchsheel Park, New Delhi – 110 017, India
Penguin Books (NZ) Ltd, Cnr Rosedale and Airborne Roads, Albany, Auckland, New Zealand
Penguin Books (South Africa) (Pty) Ltd, 5 Watkins Street, Denver Ext 4,
Johannesburg 2094, South Africa

On the World Wide Web at: www.penguin.com

Penguin Books Ltd, Registered Offices: Harmondsworth, Middlesex, England

Published in Puffin Books 1998
5

Text copyright © Steve Barlow and Steve Skidmore, 1998
Illustrations copyright © Tony Ross, 1998
All rights reserved

The moral right of the authors and illustrator has been asserted

Set in Bembo

Made and printed in England by Clays Ltd, St Ives plc

British Library Cataloguing in Publication Data
A CIP catalogue record for this book is available from the British Library

ISBN 0–140–38347–6

Contents

Chapter One
Do Drop In

"CHICKEN! CHICKEN! CHICKEN!" Perce's cry rang out across the swimming pool. "Andy's a chicken!"

Andy stared at her. There were times when he really hated Perce. This was definitely one of them.

"Look," he said, "I don't see why I'm a chicken just because I won't go to the top of the high diving board and jump off."

"Cluck, cluck, cluck …" Perce rolled on to her back and kicked out, splashing water over Andy.

"Latimer says no one is allowed to go up there."

"Since when did you start taking any notice of Latimer? Anyway, it'll liven up the lesson."

Andy had to agree; it had been a boring swimming session. The class had been churning out lengths of the local swimming pool, dressed in their pyjamas. This was called "life-saving". Perce had pointed out to Mr Latimer that if she ever did have to rescue someone from drowning, it was highly unlikely that she'd be wearing pyjamas at the time! Mr Latimer had said that wasn't the point and to stop being so stupid.

"And another thing – what am I going to wear in bed tonight?" Perce held up her dripping, chlorine-soaked pyjamas. Mr Latimer stared at Perce and walked off muttering.

But now it was free time and the rest of the class happily swam, dive-bombed each other and generally splashed about. In the deep end, Perce and Andy trod water and bickered.

"If you're so bothered about livening the lesson up, why don't you do it?"

Perce looked Andy straight in the eye. "Because I'm a girl!"

"What sort of an answer is that?"

Perce put on her superior look. "Girls don't have to show off – we know we're better than boys. Boys *have* to show off to try and make themselves look like real men. It's what boys do."

Andy was puzzled. He was sure that Perce's argument had a very large hole in it, but he couldn't quite work out what it was.

"For instance, take Well'ard," continued Perce. "Look what he got for showing off. Banned from swimming for a month." She pointed to Well'ard Wally who was sitting fully clothed on a bench at the side of the pool. He was throwing plastic bricks into the water so that other kids in the class could dive down and "rescue" them. Although more often than not, he threw the bricks *at* the other kids.

"What did he do?" asked Andy.

"Oh come on!" exclaimed Perce. "You know what happened last week."

"I was away last week."

"He had a pee in the pool!"

Andy looked incredulously at Perce. "That's not fair to ban him! Everyone knows kids pee in swimming pools."

"Yeah, but not from the high diving board!"

Andy looked in amazement at Well'ard and then up at the high diving board.

"So that's why we're banned from going up there?"

"Correct."

"What are you two arguing about?" piped up a shrill voice. Andy sculled round and saw Eddie Johnson doggy-paddling towards them.

"I've dared Andy to jump off the high diving board and he won't," explained Perce.

"You chicken!"

Andy smiled like a crocodile. "All right, Eddie, what about you doing a dare?"

There was a moment's silence as Eddie realized that he had just put his foot firmly in his big mouth. "Er ... well ... er ..." he stammered.

"Aren't you a real man?" Andy asked pointedly.

Eddie was stung into defence. "Of course I am! What do you want me to do?"

Perce burst into laughter. Not only had she hooked Andy, she'd also caught Eddie on the same hook. Boys are so stupid, she thought to herself.

Andy thought for a moment before his eyes lit up and an evil grin spread slowly across his face. "Do a double somersault off the springboard."

Eddie flinched in horror. He was useless at gymnastics. This dare was worse than jumping off the high diving board.

"Cluck, cluck …" began Perce.

"All right, I'll do it!"

"Here goes!" Eddie raced along the springboard and leapt into the air. As gravity took over, he came down, hit the end of the board hard and shot upwards.

"Geronim – OH NOOOOOOOO!"

Eddie was spun and twisted by the violence of his leap. His body performed several twists, pikes and backward rolls that would have won him an Olympic

7

gold medal if only he hadn't hit the water belly first. There was an almighty crack that echoed round the pool, and a ghastly sigh as the impact sucked air out of Eddie's body quicker than a super-turbo vacuum cleaner.

Well'ard howled with glee. "Eddie Johnson, Top of the Flops!"

Andy winced. "And now the Style marks ... zero point one, zero point three ..."

"And nine point nine from the Russian judge," added Perce.

As Eddie shot to the surface of the pool, trying desperately to gulp down lungfuls of air, everyone burst out laughing. Perce and Andy watched in hysterics as Eddie floated to the edge of the pool and hauled himself out on to the side. He then gave a lifelike impression of a recently caught fish flapping about on a river bank.

Mr Latimer strode over to Eddie.

"What do you think you're doing?"

"Uh, uh, uh," rasped Eddie.

"What?"

"Uh, uh, uh!"

Mr Latimer could see a giant purple bruise starting to appear on Eddie's stomach and took pity on him. "Come on, let's get you sorted out."

"Yuhs please, suh, uh, uh."

Mr Latimer reached down and dragged the still-flapping Eddie towards the changing rooms.

As he disappeared, Perce checked that the pool attendant was nowhere in sight. She turned to Andy. "Right, he's done his dare – now it's your turn." She pointed at the high diving board. "Up you go."

Andy peered over the edge of the board and felt dizzy. Why had he let Perce goad him into this? He was frightened of heights. He even felt sick going up an escalator.

Andy shook his head. If he had any sense, he would just step back, climb down to the safety of the ground and tell Perce that he didn't need to prove himself to her or anybody.

"Come on, you chicken!" Perce yelled from below.

Andy felt himself going hot and cold as he was hit by a nasty attack of the machos. "Right, I'll show her!" he hissed.

Taking a deep breath, he ran at the

board, leapt into space and hurtled out and downwards.

"Yeehah!" screamed Perce.

"Go, Andy!" cheered Well'ard.

Andy heard nothing but the air whizzing by. His legs thrashed wildly as he tried to gain a foothold that wasn't there.

"WHAAAAAHHHHHHHHHH..."

SPLASH!

Water shot upwards. For a few seconds, Perce was blinded as waves crashed round her head. Spluttering, she blinked the water from her eyes, and looked for Andy. There was no sign of him.

Perce began to feel worried. Perhaps Andy had hit the water awkwardly and been knocked out. Maybe she'd have to rescue him. But she wasn't even wearing pyjamas!

Telling herself not to be so stupid, Perce tried to swim towards Andy's point of entry. She found herself pushing through something that looked like snow floating on the water. She sneezed. Feathers! The surface of the pool was covered with them.

As she tried to work out what was happening, a head surged out of the depths of the pool. The spluttering figure turned to face Perce.

"Andy, what's all these …?" She recoiled in horror. The question stuck in her throat.

It wasn't Andy. It was someone else!

Chapter Two
Flying Visit

PEOPLE WERE QUEUING up to have a go at Perce.

First in line was Mr Latimer, who had stormed out of the changing rooms to find out what all the commotion was about.

"What's going on here?"

"It was Perce, sir!" Well'ard grassed. "She dared Andy to dive off the top board."

Mr Latimer went ballistic. He ranted on for ages about Irresponsible Behaviour and Ruining The Good Name Of The School (what good name? wondered Perce) and made it clear that Perce would be collecting her old-age pension before he took her swimming again.

Then there was the attendant, who had bow legs, piggy eyes and a razor haircut. He went a funny colour when he saw the mess in the pool. "Vandals!" he screamed. "Yobs! Troublemakers! Lowlife! Barbarians!" He tried to tear his hair out, but he couldn't get hold of it.

Next in to bat were the leisure-centre manager, the man who cleaned out the pool filters (now clogged with feathers), the whole of the next class who were going to have to wait for their swim while the pool was being cleared, and a lady who'd lost thirty pence in a hot-drinks machine and complained to Perce about it because everybody else was yelling at Perce so why shouldn't she?

Nobody seemed at all put out by the fact that the kid in the pool wasn't Andy.

It eventually dawned on Perce that this was because no one had noticed; except for Well'ard, who by now had dragged the strange kid out of the pool and hustled him into the changing rooms, gallantly leaving Perce to face the music.

When everyone had finished shouting at her, Perce was allowed to get changed. By the time she had struggled into her clothes and burst through the door into the foyer, Mr Latimer was already checking that no one was missing. He was moving down the line, wagging his finger to count the class. Eddie (still rubbing his stomach) winked and gave Perce a thumbs-up sign. He jerked his head sideways at the strange kid standing between himself and Well'ard.

Perce stared in disbelief. The new arrival was at least twenty centimetres taller than Andy, and broader too. She didn't know how Eddie and Well'ard had got him into Andy's clothes, but they must have used some kind of a rammer. Level Five for effort, thought Perce, but

Working Towards Level One for good thinking.

Mr Latimer reached the new kid. He stopped counting. He looked bewildered. Eventually, he cleared his throat and said, "Are you … er … all right … er … Andrew?"

"He's fine, sir," piped up Well'ard.

"I wasn't asking you, Walter."

"He can't answer you, sir." Well'ard was giving his well-known Oscar-winning performance of innocence. "He's got Laughing Jitus."

Mr Latimer was used to Well'ard. "Laryngitis."

"Yes, sir, he's got that an' all. Can't talk, sir."

Mr Latimer seemed about to argue, but when he looked at the strange kid again, his eyes glazed over; he shook his head, and went on down the line.

Perce was dying to talk to Eddie and Well'ard, and to the strange kid (assuming he *did* talk), but on the way back to school she was forced to walk next to Mr Latimer.

As soon as she got back to school, Perce was Sent For by the Head. A painful interview followed, during which the Head let it be known that she was Very Disappointed in Perce. Letters Home were mentioned. The Head also made it absolutely clear that if she had her way, Perce would suffer the death of a thousand cuts, and be boiled in oil and burned at the stake, though in what order wasn't clear.

Finally coming down from orbit, the Head pronounced sentence (loss of breaks and lunchtimes for three weeks), and told Perce that if she (the Head) heard about any more of this sort of behaviour, then she (Perce) would be Very Sorry.

At lunchtime, Perce was sitting glumly in the punishment room when there was a *psssst* noise from the direction of the window and Well'ard poked his nose over the sill.

"I heard you was in the cooler," he hissed. "How long did they give you?"

Perce glanced towards the front of the room. Miss Mills was absorbed in writing reports. Probably trying to remember how many "l's" there are in "appalling", thought Perce sourly.

From the corner of her mouth, Perce growled, "Three weeks."

"Oh well, could be worse."

"How?"

Well'ard considered for a moment. "Could have been four weeks."

"Push off, Well'ard."

Well'ard hitched himself higher. "You know that kid we pulled out of the pool? He wants to talk to you."

"*I* want to talk to *him*," snarled Perce. "Who is he?"

"Dunno really. He says his name's Icarus."

"OH, NO!"

Perce's anguished howl sent Well'ard tumbling backwards into the bushes and earned her an extra detention for making Miss Mills jab her pen clean through the report form.

★

"He was making a test flight," said Eddie.

At the end of the school day, Perce had grabbed Eddie and Well'ard. With Icarus in tow, they had made for the park to find somewhere quiet for a council of war. Perce stood facing a park bench on which the boys were sitting like the Three Wise Monkeys. She folded her arms, grimly. "Go on."

"He told us at lunchtime." Eddie indicated Icarus, who looked bewildered and apologetic. "He was trying out some new wings for his dad –"

"Dead Loss," interrupted Well'ard.

Eddie gave him a pitying look. "Dedalus," he corrected. "Only they didn't work. His dad made him jump off a cliff, and he was falling into the sea, *flap flap flap kersplash*, and then he found himself here."

"It figures." The only good thing about spending break in Solitary was that it had given Perce time to think; she had a few ideas of her own about what had happened at the swimming pool.

Icarus spoke up for the first time. "I think maybe . . ." He stopped. He had a soft, slow voice with a strange musical accent. Perce found herself wanting to hear it again.

"Go on," she said again, not quite so grimly this time.

Icarus looked up at her. "I think, maybe, we changed places. I mean, I came to where your friend was, and he went to where I was."

"Yeah?" Well'ard grunted. "Where's that then?"

"At a guess," said Perce, "Ancient Greece. About three thousand years ago . . ."

Chapter Three
Dead Loss

AS ANDY PLUNGED through the surface
of the swimming pool, a jet of water shot
up his nose nearly causing his brain to
explode. Instinct took over and he
kicked his legs to push himself up
towards the surface.

His head broke the water.

"See, Perce, I'm not a chicken!" he yelled out. "I did ..."

He stopped and looked around in wide-eyed astonishment. There was something very, very wrong.

This wasn't the local swimming pool any more, not unless:

a) someone had quickly taken the roof off to let a hot sun beat down on the water;

b) a fishing fleet had lost its way and turned up in the shallow end;

c) a rocky shoreline had been painted on the pool wall, and

d) it had been made bigger – a lot bigger. Like a few hundred square miles bigger.

Andy shook his head. I must be

dreaming, he thought. If I shut my eyes and open them again, I'll be back at the swimming pool.

So he did. But he wasn't. When he opened his eyes again, Andy was swimming in a clear blue sea off a rocky coastline, with a scorching sun beating down on him.

He began to get very worried.

"What do you think you're playing at, you stupid boy?"

"Mr Latimer?" Andy spun round in the water.

A man in a boat was heading towards him. He was dressed in a short white tunic. He had a shock of white hair. It certainly wasn't Mr Latimer. It wasn't anyone Andy knew.

"I said, what do you think you're

playing at?" The boat drifted close to Andy. The man shook his fists at him. Andy added being frightened to being worried.

"Well? Are you going to splash around enjoying yourself all day? Or are you going to get in the boat?"

It was a strange-looking boat. The planks were rough and uneven. The man stood at the back, and rowed with a single oar. As Andy struggled on board, he realized he didn't have his swimming trunks on any more – he was dressed in some sort of white loincloth.

His mind said this couldn't be happening. Unfortunately, it was being overruled by his eyes, his ears and all the rest of him.

"Where are the wings? Answer me,

you young idiot!" boomed the man.

"Wings?" spluttered Andy, wondering what he was talking about. "Erm, er ... on the birds?" he answered hopefully.

"On the birds! On the birds! What are you gabbling about, in Zeus's name? I took the feathers *off* the birds and put them *on* the wings."

Andy was losing track of the conversation. "And then you put the wings back on the birds?" he said lamely.

"NO!" yelled the man. "I put the wings on you! I, Dedalus, the greatest inventor of all time, made you a pair of wings, so you could leap off the cliff and fly in the air."

"Dedalus?" Andy flinched. The name definitely rang a bell, but only a very small one. Dedalus was pointing to something over Andy's shoulder. He turned. Andy looked up at the height of the cliff and gawped. "I jumped off there?" he trembled.

"Of course you did." Dedalus looked closely at Andy. "Don't you remember?"

Andy was pretty sure that he'd jumped off a high diving board, but he wasn't going to argue. Maybe he'd wake up soon and get out of this nightmare. He hoped so, but in the mean time, he thought he'd better humour the man who called himself Dedalus.

"Oh yes, of course. I must have banged my head when I hit the water. It's made everything go fuzzy."

Dedalus harrumphed and looked down at the water. "I suppose the wings have sunk. You couldn't even hold on to them. What sort of son are you?"

"I'm your son?" Andy was gobsmacked.

Dedalus stared at him. "Perhaps the force of the landing has scrambled your wits." He peered into Andy's eyes. "How many fingers am I holding up?"

Andy could see two, but decided to play up his "injury".

"Twenty-seven!"

"Are you sure?"

"Ah, no, sorry ... there's only twenty-six! I thought I was seeing double for a minute."

"Hmm." Dedalus looked suspiciously at Andy. "We'd better get back. We need to return to the workshop and get the spare wings ready. We don't have much time."

As Dedalus rowed back towards the shore, hundreds of thoughts flashed through Andy's head, but the one that kept coming back time and again was a growing suspicion that he was in the middle of another terrible mythological nightmare.

The boat pulled into a small harbour. Two rough-looking men looked up from the nets they were mending and sniggered.

"Well, look at that," shouted one. "Old Dedalus has caught a flying fish."

"You're wasting your time, you old crackpot!" yelled the other. "If the gods had meant us to fly, they'd have given us beaks!"

"Wings," corrected the other.

"Right! Wings!"

They fell about laughing. Dedalus snarled at them and beached the boat.

He led Andy away from the shore.

"You watch yourself, young Icarus!" called one of the men.

In the depths of Andy's memory, the small bell began to ring more loudly.

"Icarus and Dedalus?"

Suddenly, the bell started ringing like a fire alarm. "Oh no," he groaned.

He'd had visits from mythological creatures before (even though they'd never been invited). But they had come to his world. Could he now be . . . ? No, it was impossible. Surely he couldn't have?

Dedalus stopped at a long, low building and threw open a pair of rickety wooden doors. Andy peered inside and gave a gasp of astonishment. In the gloom, he could make out a long table standing in the centre of the room. Lying on it were two huge frames, one of which was partly covered in feathers. Andy realized that he was looking at a gigantic pair of half-finished wings; but they didn't look anything like the cutaway sections of wings Andy had seen in books, with spars and ribs. They were made out of some kind of thin, strong wood, woven like a basket.

"Get to work!" Dedalus pointed at the wings. "And for your own sake, make sure you do a good job."

"Why for my sake?" quavered Andy.

"Because you'll be wearing them," snarled Dedalus, "when you jump off the cliff."

Chapter Four
Pilot Error

EDDIE GAZED AT Perce in horror. "You mean . . . we're getting dragged into another Greek myth?"

"It looks like it," said Perce wearily.

"So who is this geezer?" Well'ard jerked a grimy thumb at Icarus. "One of your mythological mates, is he?"

Perce gave him a scornful glance. "Even you must have heard of the Legend of Icarus."

"Why must I? I only like legends with fighting in." Well'ard leapt off the bench and delivered a devastating Ninja attack on a rhododendron bush.

Eddie shook his head. "But why didn't Latimer notice that it wasn't Andy in the pool?"

Perce shrugged. "It's happened before. Don't you remember? With Ms Dusa, for instance. Kids were being turned to stone, and nobody even noticed that anything weird was going on. I think something happens when characters from myths start getting into our world. People get confused about what is real and what isn't."

Eddie thought hard. "You mean, when things start happening that shouldn't be happening, people pretend they aren't happening because it's easier to do that than work out what *is* happening."

Well'ard said, "I was with you right up to when you said, 'You mean' . . ."

Perce groaned. "Well'ard, a sleeping policeman's got more brains than you have. Listen, remember when we got in the Labyrinth?"

Well'ard shuddered and Eddie turned pale. They weren't likely to forget the terrifying maze in which the Minotaur (half man, half bull and all trouble) lived.

"Well," continued Perce, pointing at Icarus, "Dedalus – his dad – built it for King Minos."

Well'ard shot a dirty look at Icarus.

"Oh, did he? Must have been worth a bit of money, a big contract like that."

Icarus looked uncomfortable. "Not exactly. As soon as my father had finished building the Labyrinth, King Minos threw him into prison."

"Tough Cheddar," said Well'ard cheerfully. "Made a bodge of it, did he?"

Perce shook her head. "When Theseus went to Crete to fight the Minotaur, Dedalus helped Theseus and Ariadne find their way through the maze."

Eddie nodded. "You can see Minos would be a bit narked about that. It's like somebody selling you a really expensive bike lock, and then going and giving the combination to every bike-thief in town."

"Eventually, Minos let my father out

of prison, but he wouldn't let us leave."
Icarus sighed. "Crete is an island, so the
only way to get off was by sea, and
Minos had all the ports watched. But my
father thought of another way to
escape."

Perce looked at him steadily. "He
decided you could both fly away from
Crete."

Icarus gave her a startled look. "How
do you know?"

"Well, you see..." Perce bit her lip.
Talking to Icarus wasn't like talking to
Andy, or Eddie, or Well'ard. He didn't
seem as stupid, and Perce had a vague
feeling that she didn't want to upset him.
This was odd, because upsetting boys was
one of Perce's chief pleasures in life.

She tried again. "You see, all this stuff

with you and your dad . . . it all happened a long time ago. So long ago that people aren't sure whether it really happened or not. It's a legend, to us."

"The Legend of Icarus," said Eddie. "That sounds familiar." He began to go cross-eyed with the effort of remembering.

"We've had visits from . . . people from legends before." Perce didn't somehow feel this was quite the moment to tell Icarus that their earlier visitors had generally wanted to get rid of her and Andy in various nasty ways. "We don't even know exactly where they come from, whether it's the past . . . our past, I mean . . . or whether there's a sort of World of Myth where things are . . . well, different," she finished lamely.

Icarus thought for a moment, and then said, "This legend you're talking about…" He hesitated. "Does it have a … happy ending?"

Perce felt her mouth going dry. "Why do you ask?"

"It's just that my father's plans haven't worked very well. I've tried lots of wings for him, and none of them works. Every time, he says that I must jump from a higher place so the wings have more time to work." He looked up at Perce. "I thought I was going to die when I fell today. Sooner or later —"

"Got it!" Eddie snapped his fingers. "I do know this one! You see, what happens is, your dad makes these wings that *do* work, and you fly off over the sea …"

"Eddie," hissed Perce warningly.

". . . only you fly too close to the sun, and the wax holding the feathers on your wings melts . . ."

"Eddie, shut up!"

". . . and you fall in the sea and drown." Eddie looked from Icarus's stricken face to Perce's vicious scowl. "Was it something I said?"

Perce turned to Icarus. "Don't worry, it's not going to happen." She realized she was gabbling and forced herself to speak calmly. "It's just a story. Anyway, nothing like that can happen to you while you're here, can it?"

"It can to Andy though." There was an odd quiver in Eddie's voice. "If Icarus has come out of the legend and turned up here, then this Dedalus bloke is going to be looking for a new test-pilot, isn't he?

And if you two are right and Andy has gone into the legend ..."

Perce groaned and collapsed on to the bench. "Then it will be Andy who falls into the sea and drowns!"

Chapter Five
Flight Plan

THE PROBLEM OF finding Icarus somewhere to stay had been solved quite simply. Perce had walked Icarus back to Andy's house. When she had opened the door, Andy's mum had looked surprised for a moment; but then Perce had pushed Icarus into the house, and called out, "Goodnight, Andy," and that had been that.

"She stared at me a few times," Icarus told Perce the next morning as they walked to school. "She looked a bit puzzled, but after a while she seemed just to … accept me." He shrugged.

The first session for Perce's class was science. As luck would have it, the current topic was flight. Although he'd missed the first week of the project, Icarus was fascinated by Mr Latimer's explanation about wing shapes, and the way that air flowed over them to create lift. He watched a video about gliding with shining eyes. (Even Perce had enjoyed that bit of the lesson. It looked fun.)

At break, Perce found that it was Mr Latimer's turn to supervise the detention.

"Sit down, Priscilla!"

Perce squirmed inside. She hated to be called by her real name, but she arranged her face in a sweet smile. (Look Number Three for dealing with teachers: "Open and Innocent".)

"And what are you grinning like that for? You look like a blasted gargoyle." Mr Latimer was missing his morning snack. His hands were twitching – a sure sign of Bikkie Withdrawal Syndrome, thought Perce. Anyway, look who was calling her a gargoyle! She let the smile fade and tried Look Number Seven: "Serious and Attentive".

"Please, sir . . ."

"Have you brought any work to do? If not, I'm sure I can find you some."

"Yes I have, sir," lied Perce. "I've brought my science project. The one we're doing on aero-thingy … you know, sir, flying."

"Aerodynamics."

"Yes, sir, only I need some help."

Mr Latimer wasn't feeling helpful. He didn't want to supervise Perce, who was the only pupil on punishment. He wanted to be in the staffroom with a nice cup of coffee and a chocolate digestive. "If you need to know something, you'll have to look it up."

Old misery, thought Perce. Aloud, she said, "But I'm not allowed out of the punishment room, sir."

Mr Latimer groaned. "Go on, then."

"Well, sir, is it possible for people to fly? I mean, not in a plane or anything, just fly by themselves?"

"No."

Perce waited patiently. She knew Mr Latimer wouldn't be able to leave it at that; he was a teacher, after all. Teachers needed to explain things.

"Well, people can glide of course, with the right equipment, but they have to start from somewhere high up. But real flying... no. People are too heavy. Their muscles aren't strong enough."

"But what about Icarus, sir? He flew, didn't he?"

"Poppycock!" Mr Latimer tended to get overheated when discussing Greek myths. "That's just a legend. Firstly, in real life, Icarus and Dedalus would never have got off the ground. Secondly, if Icarus had flown towards the sun, the air would have got colder as he gained height, not hotter, so the wax on his wings wouldn't have melted ..." He stopped and threw Perce a suspicious glance. "Why this sudden interest in mythology, anyway? Nothing's ... happened, has it?"

"Oh no, sir," lied Perce with a bright smile. "Nothing at all."

Dedalus's workshop was hopelessly cluttered. Strange-looking tools lay where they had been dropped. Dozens of clay pots, hundreds of pieces of metal, string and rope were scattered about, filling the room from floor to ceiling. It looked like a scrapyard after a hurricane.

Dedalus dug a double handful of feathers from a bag in the corner, sneezed violently, and shambled over to where Andy sat slumped in exhaustion.

"Come on, then! What are you waiting for?" The old man put the feathers down, crossed to his fire, and lifted a pot of newly melted wax from it. He brought it over to Andy. "The wings, boy, the wings!"

Andy looked at the wings in confusion. "But I've finished them, haven't I? I mean, there aren't any gaps or anything ..."

"Oh, yes!" roared Dedalus. "You'd like that, wouldn't you! One pair of wings! One! So you can fly off and leave your old dad behind, is that the idea? Oh no, my boy ..." With an effort, Dedalus lifted the finished wings off the table. "We go together!"

Stacking the covered wings against the wall, the old man took down a second set of woven frames. Andy gazed at them in horror. It had taken him most of the night to finish the first set! As Dedalus lifted the new frames on to the table, there was a terrific banging at the door. Someone outside bellowed, "Open! In the name of King Minos!"

Dedalus gave a gasp of terror. All the bad temper and bluster seemed to drain out of him. He scuttled over to the door and opened it, practically grovelling to the two men who came in. They were big men with jaws like anvils. They wore armour and carried spears.

They looked around the workshop

while Dedalus bowed and cringed. One of them turned suddenly and thrust the point of his spear to within a centimetre of Dedalus's nose. The old man went cross-eyed staring at the sharp tip.

The soldier gave an evil smile. "King Minos is very disappointed."

"Yeah, disappointed," repeated the other soldier.

"He only let you out of the Labyrinth," the first soldier went on, "because you promised to build him a flying ship . . ."

"Yeah, ship."

". . . and that was weeks ago, so now he wants to know, what's the hold-up?"

"Yeah, hold-up?"

Dedalus waved his hands about. "Boys, boys, I promise you, I'm working on it;

these things take time! I did a test just yesterday . . ."

"And did it work?"

"Yeah, work?"

"Well, not exactly, but next time . . ."

The man with the spear moved his lips. He may have thought he was smiling. "Next time, it'd better work. King Minos says you got two days. If you're not ready by then–" He made a throat-cutting gesture – "you'll be for the high jump. Geddit? High jump!" He roared with laughter.

"Yeah, the long jump. Hur hur hur."

The first soldier stopped laughing and gave the second a dirty look. "Long jump? Are you stupid?"

"Yeah, stupid."

"Come on!" The two soldiers went

out, breaking a few things on the way.

Dedalus shut the door behind them and leaned against it, panting. "Get to work! You heard them. If we're not ready in two days, they'll throw us both off the cliff!" He glared at Andy. "Without wings!"

Chapter Six
A Touch of Flew

EDDIE ROCKED GENTLY back and forth on a swing. "I've got a plan," he chirped.

"Oh yeah?" sneered Perce.

"Yeah. Simple. We think Andy went back to where Icarus came from when he came here, so all we've got to do is find some way to send Icarus back from here to there at the same time as bringing Andy back from there to here, if he's there in the first place!"

"Nice plan," replied Perce sarcastically. "How do we do that, then?"

"I haven't thought of that bit yet. Give me a chance!"

Perce looked at Icarus. "Anyway, we can't send Icarus back."

Well'ard sat on the monkey bars scratching his head, making several fleas homeless. "Why not?" he asked. "Anyway, why do we have to think of a plan? Why can't the Greek geek over there come up with one?"

Perce clenched her fists. "He's not a geek. And we can't send him back because his dad will kill him with his daft inventions. Anyway, he's not like the other mythological nutters we've met. He's nice and ..." Perce tailed off as Well'ard and Eddie stared hard at her.

"You fancy 'im!" hooted Well'ard.

"No, I don't," denied Perce.

"Yes you do! You're going red!"

Perce felt a blush spreading over her cheeks. "I must be coming down with flu," she muttered lamely.

"Perhaps you caught it off him," said Eddie pointing at Icarus. "He 'flu' here!" Well'ard and Eddie both fell about barking with laughter.

Perce felt embarrassed. Why shouldn't she like Icarus? For a boy, he was all right. Mind you, she'd never let on that she thought so. Not to anyone. No way!

Eddie took a break from barking like a

demented seal to whisper in Well'ard's ear. Well'ard began to guffaw and nodded at Eddie.

"Hey, Perce, what are your favourite sweets?" Eddie asked innocently.

"Why?"

"I bet they're . . . Icarus Allsorts!" Eddie and Well'ard fell about in even greater fits of laughter.

"Right! Enough's enough!" Perce grabbed Eddie by his collar and put her fist up against his mouth.

"Actually, Eddie, my favourite sweets are *gobstoppers*! Now, are you going to cut out the stupid comments?"

Eddie and Well'ard nodded dumbly. This was more like the Perce they knew and loved, or, more accurately, knew and didn't love.

"Now," said Perce calmly, "we need a proper plan."

"Why don't we ask Liquorice?" said Well'ard. "Maybe he's got a plan."

Icarus looked up. "I think I shall need my wings."

"But they're broken," protested Perce. "Anyway, I told you. I asked Latimer and he says people can't fly."

"Not here, they can't." Eddie thought hard. "Where Icarus comes from, it might be different. If there are creatures that can turn people to stone, or are half human and half bull, flying should be a doddle!"

Perce nodded decisively. "In that case, we'll have to build some new wings. What are they made of?"

"Steel," said Well'ard confidently.

"Well'ard, how can you be so stupid

with only one head? We're not talking about aeroplane wings!"

Icarus spoke up. "My father makes wings from wooden frames covered with feathers."

Well'ard grinned. "I know where we can get some feathers."

"Good." Perce pointed at Well'ard. "You and Eddie go and get them. Icarus and I will sort out the frames. And hurry! Andy could be in terrible danger."

"He'll be all right," said Eddie, trying to reassure everyone. "He's probably having a great time, lazing about on a beach getting a nice suntan or something …"

"Get a move on, you idle creature, or I'll

flog you until your back bleeds!" Dedalus was standing over Andy holding a thick cane.

"Why have I got to do all the work?" Andy asked, picking a pile of feathers up.

"Because, ah . . . aah . . . aaah aaaachoo! Because I'm allergic to feathers. I sneeze and come out in rashes."

"Well, I'm allergic to work," muttered Andy. "I yawn and come out in tiredness."

"Don't be insolent, boy!" boomed Dedalus. "You heard King Minos's men – we only have two more days to build his ship."

"But you're not building a ship!"

"Exactly. That's why we have to build the wings, leap off the cliff and fly to our freedom before they return. Achoo!"

Andy looked down at the wings. He'd been sticking feathers on to the frames for hours. I wish I had a tube of Superglue, he thought.

Dedalus looked carefully at Andy's work. "This side of the frame is covered. We need to turn the wing over. Help me lift it ..."

Andy's jaw dropped. Inspiration hit him like a snowball down the earhole. That was what was wrong! That's why Dedalus's wings wouldn't work.

"Lift!" he shouted. "That's it! Lift!"

Dedalus stared at him. "Yes ... lift. Pick ... It ... Up ... And ... Lift."

"No, I mean that's what you need. That's why you haven't been able to fly.

The wings should be curved, like a bird's. That's what gives them lift."

Dedalus shook his head. "Mad. The boy's gone mad."

"No, I haven't! These wings are straight. The aerodynamics are wrong."

Dedalus looked puzzled. "The hairy dry manics? What are they?"

"Aerodynamics ... they're ... dynamics ... of air." Andy wished he hadn't fallen asleep during that bit of the science lesson.

Dedalus spluttered with rage. "Are you trying to tell me, the greatest inventor the world has ever seen, that you know more about the science of flight than I do?"

"We're doing it at school."

"School? What's school?"

Andy realized that schools hadn't been

invented yet. Well'ard should be here, he thought, he'd be in heaven!

"It doesn't matter. The wings have got to be curved." Dedalus shook his head angrily. "Look," Andy went on, "even if I'm wrong, nothing you've tried so far has worked. What have you got to lose?"

Dedalus stood in silence for a long time, biting his lip. Eventually he spread his hands. "All right. Curved. We'll try it." He glowered at Andy. "So you'd better get working even harder. We must be ready to escape."

Andy nodded. "I'm right about the curved wings. You'll see."

"Oh, I shall." Dedalus gave him a wicked grin. "Because when we jump off the cliff, you go first."

Chapter Seven
Feathered Friends

"ARE YOU SURE this will work?" asked
Eddie as he watched Well'ard ripping
up pieces of bread and throwing them
on the ground. The trail of bread led
from the park lake to a large clump of
bushes.

"Course it will," replied Well'ard. "The stupid ducks will eat the bread and then we nab 'em with this." He held up a landing net which he had nicked from his dad's fishing kit. "The SAS do this to survive in the desert," he continued.

Eddie thought for a moment. "But there's no ducks in the desert," he pointed out.

"That's cos the SAS caught them all." Well'ard threw down the last scrap of bread and settled himself in a large rhododendron bush. "You doubtin' me?"

"No ..." said Eddie, doubting him.

"Well, come 'ere and get ready to pluck duck!"

For the next hour, Eddie crouched next to Well'ard, ready to grab any unsuspecting ducks that had taken the bait. His fingers ached from gripping the landing net and cramp had begun to set in his leg.

"How long do we have to wait?" he hissed.

"For as long as it takes." Well'ard's face was set hard with determination. "Sometimes the SAS wait for days."

"But I've got to be home for tea."

"Wimp! You'd never survive in the desert."

"I'm not in the desert. I'm in a bush in the park …"

"Shhh!" hissed Well'ard. "Hear that?"

There was a scratching noise coming from round the corner. "We've got one!" Well'ard's voice squeaked in excitement. "Get the net ready."

Eddie obeyed and raised the net.

"Come on, duck ..." whispered Well'ard, eyes ablaze with anticipation.

"Sniff, sniff."

A seed of doubt began to grow in Eddie's mind. "Sniff, sniff?" He was sure ducks didn't sniff.

"Well'ard ... ?"

"Shhhh! Get ready ..."

"But ..." The seed had grown into a medium-sized garden centre.

"SSHHHH! It's nearly here ... ready, Eddie ... GO!"

Well'ard and Eddie leapt out and threw the net.

After a moment's pause, Eddie said in a very flat sort of voice, "Well'ard ... you know about ducks, don't you?"

"Erm ... yeah."

"Are there any ducks that have fur?"

"Erm ..."

"Are there any ducks that growl?"

"Well ..."

"Are there any ducks that are as big as a sheep and have got four legs and very large teeth?"

"Ah ... no."

"Then I think what we've got here is an Alsatian."

"GRRRRRRR ..."

"RUN!"

An hour later Well'ard and Eddie were back at the side of the lake. Their clothes were tattered from their encounter with the four-legged, bushy-tailed "duck". Nevertheless, a few scratches, bite marks and torn clothes weren't enough to deter

Well'ard. He eyed the ducks happily swimming on the lake.

"Right, time for Plan B."

Eddie rubbed his backside. "I hope it's better than Plan A. That dog bit me right on the –"

"Stop moaning," ordered Well'ard. "This time we creep up on that load of ducks."

"Flock."

"What?"

"You mean a flock of ducks. It's a collective noun," explained Eddie.

Well'ard just stood staring blankly.

"It's a term given to the name of a group of things," continued Eddie.

Well'ard continued staring blankly.

"For instance, you have a herd of cattle or a flight of birds ... a brood of chickens ..."

"Eddie, shut it."

". . . a shrewdness of apes . . . an unkindness of ravens . . . a murder of crows . . ."

Well'ard grabbed Eddie's torn collar.

"If you don't shut it, there'll be an
unkindness of me and a murder of
Eddie."

Eddie shut up.

"Right. We'll have that one." Well'ard
pointed to a duck which had wandered
away from the lake and was nonchalantly
pecking at the grass. "It's duck-pluckin'
time!"

Eddie watched as Well'ard took what
was left of the landing net and began to
tiptoe towards the duck.

"Here, ducky, ducky," Well'ard
whispered. "Come to Uncle Well'ard . . ."

Eddie held his breath as Well'ard got

closer to the duck.

"Do you feel lucky, ducky?"

The duck stopped pecking at the ground. Well'ard stopped dead in his tracks.

"Come on, duck, make my day!" The duck turned and, instead of flying off, craned its neck, beat its wings and advanced on the two "hunters".

"Er ... what's up, duck?"

"QUACK!"

"RUN!"

"Plan C is bound to work."

Eddie was not convinced. He and Well'ard had returned to the lake after being chased across the park by the mad duck and its mates. Their clothes were even more tattered.

"What's Plan C?" asked Eddie.

"We forget the creeping up bit. Look, there's a duck just the other side of those bushes. You can see its feathers."

Eddie was too battered and bruised to argue. He just nodded his head weakly.

"So what we do is, we dive through the bushes and grab it before it knows what's happenin'. Surprise attack, right? One, two, three …"

They dived through the bushes. Well'ard reached out blindly, grabbed and yanked hard. He held up his hand in triumph.

"Free!" he gloated. "I got free feathers…"

"Well'ard …"

Well'ard turned. Eddie was standing stock still and pointing a trembling finger.

"That isn't a duck. That's a swan."

Well'ard eyed the large white form. "So? It's still got feathers."

"A swan can break a person's arm with its wing," quivered Eddie as he slowly backed away. "Swans are vicious. Especially when they get annoyed."

"Do you reckon it looks annoyed?" asked Well'ard.

"You've just pulled three feathers off its tenderest bit. What do you think?"

"HISS!"

"RUN!"

"Three feathers! Is that all you've got? We need thousands!"

Perce was unimpressed by Well'ard and Eddie's adventures. Even Icarus had laughed at their description of the attack of the killer duck.

"You ran away from a duck?" sneered Perce. "Was it a well'ard mallard?"

"It bit me," protested Well'ard.

"Ducks don't have teeth, they have bills," replied Perce curtly.

"Well, it billed me, then."

Perce shook her head. "Pathetic, absolutely pathetic."

"Well," huffed Eddie, "if you're going to be like that you can get your own feathers."

Well'ard nodded in agreement.

"Come, Well'ard, we're obviously not wanted here." Eddie stalked off. "I have a better idea. I know how we can save Andy ..."

Chapter Eight
Bird Brains

ICARUS FINISHED TIGHTENING a screw and stepped back to admire his handiwork. "Done!"

He and Perce had spent the whole of Saturday in Perce's garage, working on the new wings. The frame of the left-hand wing lay across the workbench. The right-hand frame lay wobbling across the handle of the lawnmower and the back of a folding garden chair. Perce glued another feather on to it, then turned round.

They were working from plans for a model aeroplane kit (which Perce's dad had bought but never found the time to make up). Once Icarus had got the idea from the drawings, there had been no stopping him. All the tools in the garage were unfamiliar to him, especially the powered ones, but he was a quick learner. Before long he was exclaiming delightedly at the speed with which the electric saw cut shapes out of plywood (which Perce's dad had bought for some do-it-yourself work in the loft). The first frame had been completed using thin strips of wood (which Perce's dad had bought for fixing the plywood *to*), and covered with shade netting.

"Oh goodie. Another wing to cover." Perce turned back to her work and carefully glued another feather on to the frame. "Seven thousand, four hundred and thirty-three," she said wearily. She picked up another feather and dabbed a spot of glue on the end. "Seven thousand, four hundred and ..."

Icarus came and looked over her shoulder. "We should be using wax," he complained.

Perce shook her head. "You can't get hold of wax that easily these days, not unless you fancy digging around in Well'ard's ears. Anyway, this is the latest stuff. Sticks anything. And it won't melt if it gets hot."

"Where did you get the feathers from, anyway?"

"You don't want to know."

"I do. That's why I asked."

"When I say you don't want to know," Perce explained, "I mean you may want to know, but if you did know, you wouldn't want to, and in this case, believe me, you *really* don't want to know."

As Icarus was still trying to puzzle this out, a thunderous banging shook the garage door. Perce went across and opened it. Outside, Eddie and Well'ard were leaning on their bikes.

"What do you want?" demanded Perce sourly. "I thought you weren't helping any more."

"Well, that's all you know, see," sneered Well'ard. "We ain't been wasting our time like you have. We done the business."

Eddie was beside himself with excitement. "Come on!" He grabbed Perce by the sleeve. "We've got something to show you."

Perce shook him off. "What could you bozos have to show us?"

Well'ard waved his hand in the air. "*Only* the answer to all your boyfriend's problems ..."

"He is *not* my boyfr—"

"*Only* the thing that's going to get Andy back." Well'ard looked even more smug. "Job done. Sorted!"

Perce put her hands on her hips. "Listen, you turkeys, if you think I'm going to drop everything and get roped in to one of your hare-brained schemes ..."

"PERCE!"

"... you're absolutely right!" Perce grabbed her bike and leapt on it. As she pedalled furiously away, she could still hear her mother calling after her ...

"Perce! Where are you going? Have you seen my best duvet?"

Perce gazed at the contraption. "What is it?"

"Hang-glider," said Eddie proudly. "Me and Well'ard made it."

"Yeah," smirked Well'ard. "While you an' loverboy were messin' about with feathers, we built this. Took us nearly all night."

Perce leant on her handlebars. She

hadn't much idea what went into the construction of a hang-glider, but she was pretty sure it didn't include a clothes horse, aluminium curtain track or rather nasty pink nylon bed sheets. Eddie's creation looked like a kite that had been in a road smash with a television aerial.

Icarus stood beside Perce, panting. This wasn't surprising: he didn't have a bike, and had run all the way. "What is it?" he asked. "A windmill?"

Perce turned to stare at Eddie. "I thought you said you had a plan to save Andy."

"We have!" Eddie was indignant. "All Liquorice has got to do is strap himself in here and put on the rollerblades, get up a bit of speed down the hill, and hey presto!"

"Yeah, hey presto sudden death. Eddie, you're out of your tree."

"Come on, there's nothing to worry about." Eddie reached inside his backpack and pulled out a flying helmet and a pair of goggles. He offered them to Icarus, who shook his head and backed away.

"Tell you what," said Perce. "You show us."

Eddie gulped. "Me?"

Perce and Icarus watched with interest as Eddie and Well'ard went through the final pre-flight checks.

"Contact!"

"Contact who?" asked Eddie. "You mean, phone them or something?"

Well'ard looked baffled. "I dunno, it's

just what they say in films before they take off."

Eddie straightened his goggles. "OK, what's next?"

"Chocks away!" Well'ard reached into Eddie's pocket and whipped out a Chocolate Yummy Bar.

"Hey, what are you doing with that?"

"Well, you don't want it to get squashed, do you?"

"Look, I'm not sure this is such a good idea …"

"Wilco! Roger! Over and out!" Well'ard gave Eddie a good hard shove. With a stifled squeak, Speedbird Eddie set off down the runway.

The rollerblades rumbled on the Tarmac road surface. Eddie's contraption swayed and wobbled alarmingly. Bits began to flap loose.

Hopping up and down in excitement, Well'ard cupped his hands in front of his mouth and yelled, "Rotate!"

Eddie was really getting up speed now. From far away, they heard him scream: "What? Turn round, at this speed? You must be mad!"

"It means take off!" bellowed Well'ard. "Take off!"

Perce and Icarus watched open-mouthed as Eddie's feet left the ground ...

Chapter Nine
Flights of Fancy

ANDY SNORED. HE was asleep on a pile of feathers. They weren't as comfortable as they looked. They tickled.

He and Dedalus had spent most of the night trying to put a curve in the wings. Eventually, Dedalus had decided that the easiest way to do this was to soak the wings, and bend them while they were wet. This had meant several trips down to the beach, carrying the wings to dip them in the sea. Also, most of the feathers had come off in the water and had to be collected. Andy had fallen asleep while Dedalus was working on the frames.

"Wake up, you idle dog!"

A vicious kick sent Andy sprawling. He looked up to see Dedalus standing over him, scowling.

"What was that for?" he complained.

"You haven't time to lie about!" Dedalus jerked his thumb at the wings. Andy looked at them, and groaned.

A few pitiful feathers still clung to the frames, but the rest were lying in scattered heaps round the workshop, wet and bedraggled.

Dedalus kicked Andy again. "Get back to work. All these feathers – Achoo! – have got to be dried. Then you've got two pairs of wings to cover."

Andy groaned. "I'm sick of sticking feathers! I don't care if the stupid wings never get finished."

"Would you rather be hurled from a terrible height and fall screaming to a horrific death on jagged rocks?"

Andy thought for a moment. "Good point, well made." He reached for the pot of wax.

Eddie took to the air. He sailed over a hedge. He defied gravity, he rose like a swan, he flew ...

. . . like a brick.

Eddie came to earth with the sort of noise you might get if you had an attack of wind while sitting in a bath full of yoghurt.

As Well'ard set off down the hill at a sprint, Perce plucked a blade of grass and chewed it. "Good job the farmer decided to put his manure pile just there. Nice soft landing. Mind you, it looks a bit squishy."

Icarus looked concerned. "Do you think we should help them?" he asked, without enthusiasm.

"Nah."

Below them, Well'ard was trying to pull Eddie from the heap by his feet. He was finding this difficult as he was trying to hold his nose at the same time.

Perce turned her bike round with a sigh. "Come on. We'd better get back to gluing feathers. Maybe Mum will have calmed down a bit by now ..."

She suddenly became aware that Icarus hadn't moved. A shadow passed over her. She turned. Icarus was staring up into the sky, entranced.

Perce looked up. A hang-glider soared effortlessly across the face of the hill. Catching an updraught, it began to climb in a lazy spiral. Icarus stared at it with longing in his eyes.

"It can be done," he whispered. "Human beings can fly."

Perce put down her bike and stood beside him. "You remember Latimer going on about warm air currents? Whadjamacallums, thermals. He's found one. He's using it to gain height. That's the secret. You don't fight the wind, you use it." She watched the glider climb steadily. "They don't often come over here – he must have flown miles!"

Icarus licked his lips. "With one of those, I could jump off the highest cliff with no fear. I could escape from Crete. I could escape from my father!"

Perce shook her head regretfully. "Forget it. They cost thousands of pounds."

Icarus looked crestfallen.

Shielding her eyes, Perce gazed towards the distant hills where the hang-gliders launched. She could just make out two or three of the graceful swallow-winged shapes ... and a dumpier, mushroom-shaped glider some way below them that seemed to swing like a pendulum. That would be a parascender, a gliding parachute. A parachute ...

"Yes!" Perce punched the air. Icarus turned a startled face to her. "Listen, no time to explain. Help Well'ard get Eddie out. Get them both to help you finish the wings. See you later."

Pedalling furiously, Perce covered the ten miles to the local airfield in forty minutes.

The instructor from the parachute training school rubbed his chin. "Well, I dunno. For school, you said?"

Perce held her breath. She knew that the drama club at the comprehensive school had a parachute. They had brought it to Perce's school for a workshop.

"What school is it?"

Perce told him. The instructor brightened. "Hey, yeah? Is old Latimer still there?"

"Er ... yes."

"He used to be my teacher. I reckon it was him that got me interested in skydiving. I mean, after you've been hauled over the coals a few times by old Latimer, jumping out of an aeroplane at several thousand metres doesn't seem like any big deal."

Perce nodded. She knew what he meant.

"I think I can do something for you. We've got a few old 'chutes we were going to hire out to a film company, but the film got cancelled." The instructor disappeared into a storeroom and came out carrying something that looked like a floppy rucksack. "Well, this one's all packed up and ready to go. We're sending the old stuff out to schools and charities next week, but you can have it now if you like. Are you going to do some drama with it, then?"

Perce picked up the pack and smiled. "If things work out all right, I reckon it could be pretty dramatic."

Chapter Ten
Fly Away Home

THE FOLLOWING EVENING, Perce peered cautiously through the doorway from the changing room. The pool was deserted.

She had hidden in a cubicle until the changing rooms emptied. Now she crept round the edge of the pool to the fire exit, opened it and whistled.

Eddie and Well'ard scampered out from the bushes carrying the finished wings. Icarus followed more slowly with a large bundle. Perce pulled the fire door shut behind them.

"Right," she hissed, "they'll be turning the alarms on in a few minutes. Let's get cracking." Icarus looked around, undecided. "Look, you'll have the parachute. It'll work. Trust me."

Icarus gazed at her for a moment, then nodded and started to peel off the tracksuit he'd borrowed from Andy's wardrobe. At a signal from Perce, Eddie (who still niffed a bit from yesterday's crash landing) and Well'ard started to climb the steps to the top diving board, hauling the wings up with them.

Finishing the wings had taken the whole day, even with all four of them gluing feathers. The results were pretty impressive. The wings were light, and seemed strong enough. They looked terrific; but would they fly?

Perce lifted the pack on to Icarus's back, and helped him adjust the harness. "This is the ripcord. Pull it if the wings don't work, and the parachute will open out."

Icarus nodded.

"If the wings do work, then you can still use the parachute to get away from your father. You climb as high as you can, and . . ."

"Yes, I remember. It's a good plan. Thank you."

Well'ard appeared at Perce's elbow. "We put the wings on the platform. All he's gotta do is strap 'em on and jump off yelling 'Bonsai!'"

Perce rolled her eyes. "Banzai."

"Whatever. Shall we help him get the wings on?"

"I'll do it. You watch the doors."

"Want to give him a goodbye kiss, do you?" Well'ard saw Perce's fists clench. "Tell you what, I'll watch the doors."

Perce turned to Icarus. "Come on."

They started to climb towards the platform.

Andy stood on top of the cliff. The afternoon sun beat down on him. He shivered. How had he got into this mess?

97

What was he doing here? Why didn't he just run away?

He felt the point of Dedalus's dagger jab into his back. Ah yes, that was the reason.

Dedalus's harsh voice grated in his ear. "What are you waiting for? Jump."

Andy looked down. He felt his head swimming. Far, far below, the sea crashed on to wicked-looking rocks. "Look, the doctor says I mustn't go jumping off cliffs because it might bring on a nasty attack of getting killed, also I've got a verruca, my mum gave me a note ..."

"Stop your foul whining!" Dedalus brought his knife up to Andy's throat. "Jump!"

"After you."

Dedalus snorted. "You cry baby! What

are you making such a fuss about? It's one small step for a man …"

"No it isn't! It's a giant leap with lots of 'aaarrrgh' and a 'splat' at the end!"

The knife hovered a millimetre from Andy's belly button. "If you don't jump, the crows shall feast on your living entrails."

"Well, since you ask so nicely …"

Andy gulped.

He spread his wings and stepped off the cliff.

"Mummmmmmeeeeeeeeeee!"

Out of control, with wings flapping madly, Andy hurtled towards certain death on the rocks below.

Perce pulled the last strap on the wings tight. She glanced down at the unnaturally clear and glassy surface of the empty pool. "That's it, then. Remember, don't fight the air. Use it." She looked up. Icarus was staring straight into her eyes.

Perce suddenly felt very hot and very small.

"Look, maybe this isn't such a good idea," she said in a slightly shaky voice. "Perhaps there's another way of getting Andy back ..."

"No. This is the only way." Icarus looked at her steadily. "Thank you for all you've done."

"But what if the wings don't work? What if —"

"If the wings don't work, maybe the parachute will." Icarus shrugged. "I think I have a much better chance now than I did when I came here. What happens, the gods will decide."

He paused, and smiled slightly. Then he leant forward, just a little.

He's going to kiss me, thought Perce. Hooray! Help!

She closed her eyes.

When she opened them again, Icarus was gone.

Chapter Eleven
Splashdown

IT SEEMED TO Icarus that a thousand stars
had exploded and lit up every corner of
his brain. He screwed his eyes shut. When
they blinked open, the harsh neon light of
the swimming pool had been transformed
into bright blinding sunlight. As he

tumbled helplessly through the air, Icarus glimpsed the figure of his father peering over the edge of the cliff. The plan had worked, he was back!

The feeling of relief quickly vanished as Icarus realized he was plunging towards the rocks below. He began to panic and tried to flap his arms. It was no good, he couldn't! His wings were being pushed upwards by the force of the air. He was going to die.

A huge splash echoed round the pool.

Perce half ran, half slid down the steps. She reached the poolside. Eddie and Well'ard stood gazing dumbly at the water. Waves splashed over their feet. The whole surface of the pool was smothered with feathers.

Perce grabbed the long pole that the instructors used to tow beginners. She fished around under the surface. She felt the pole poke into something soft.

With an eruption of feathers, a head broke the surface. Well'ard and Eddie burst into loud cheers.

Perce breathed a sigh of relief. "Welcome back, Andy." She put her hands on her hips. "Well? Are you going to splash around enjoying yourself all day?"

By the time the piggy-eyed attendant arrived, his howls of rage echoed round a deserted pool. Thousands of feathers danced on its ruffled surface, and an open fire door swung gently in the breeze.

★

As Icarus closed his eyes and waited for the inevitable sickening crunch, a familiar female voice from across the centuries seemed to whisper in his ear.

"Don't fight the air. Use it."

With a muscle-wrenching effort, Icarus pulled his arms down and held them out horizontally. Spray from the crashing waves stung his face. The rocks got nearer and nearer as Icarus stretched out for his life and shouted out Perce's advice.

"Don't fight the air! USE IT!"

As if obeying his demand, air billowed under the wings and lifted Icarus out of the death dive. He began to glide up and away from the body-tearing waves and brain-splitting rocks.

He was doing it! He was flying!

"It works!" Icarus heard his father's triumphant cry from the cliff top. "I knew it would! I am a genius!"

Icarus soared gleefully along the cliff edge. All right, Father, he thought. It's your turn to jump now, see how you like it. Let's see you fly. And then ... catch me if you can. He laughed out loud. His wings carried him aloft like a bird ... no, like a god! He was invincible! He could do anything!

Dedalus watched Icarus soaring away, gliding and swooping on the currents of hot air.

"Well done, my boy! Farewell, Minos! Farewell, Crete!" chuckled Dedalus as he strapped on his pair of wings and made his way to the cliff's edge. He looked down towards the rocks ... and hesitated.

There was a big difference between ordering Icarus to jump off the cliff and doing it himself. What if the wings didn't work? After all he was heavier than his son and anyway . . .

"Oi, Dedalus, where do you think you're goin'?"

"Yeah, goin'?"

Looking down, Icarus saw two men with his father. They were wearing the uniform of King Minos's guard. Both held drawn bows, with the arrows pointing straight at Dedalus. Fear surged through Icarus. Although his father spent every waking hour inventing new ways of putting him in danger, he didn't want to see Dedalus made into a pincushion.

"You're dead, Dedalus."

"Yeah, Dead-alas. Hur hur."

There was no escape for Dedalus. Even if he tried to fly away, the archers could hardly miss.

A shadow passed over him. He looked up. Minos's men screamed and dropped their bows, flinging themselves to the ground as Icarus swooped towards them. "Jump, Father!"

Dedalus jumped.

The shocked henchmen crawled to the cliff's edge and peered over to watch the crazed inventor plummet to his doom. Then they gasped in amazement as Dedalus swooped up and flew away from the rocks, the waves, his island prison and King Minos.

"See, my boy! What a genius I am!" As they flew further from Crete, Icarus could hear Dedalus crowing triumphantly behind him. The old man was full of himself. "And when we reach the mainland, I can continue with my experiments. There are many more things for me to invent and for you to try out! I have so many ideas: ships that can sail underwater, chariots that move without horses, shoes with wheels on. I can see them now!" He chuckled. "And you, Icarus, will have the honour of testing them out. You are going to have a great deal of fun!"

More like a great deal of bruises and broken bones, thought Icarus. They were flying over a smooth sea studded with small islands. Crete lay far behind them. It was time to put Perce's plan into action.

Icarus began to climb higher into the sky; further away from Dedalus and nearer to the sun.

"What are you doing, you fool?" A note of panic crept into Dedalus's voice. "You're going too high! The wax on your wings will melt!"

That's what I want you to think, grinned Icarus. He flew higher, straight towards the sun. Even so, it was getting colder, just as Perce had told him it would.

Dedalus squinted upwards to where Icarus had disappeared into the blinding glare of the sun. "Where are you, boy? I can't see you!"

Good, thought Icarus. Then it's time.

He unstrapped his wings and flung them away. As he dropped from the sky,

Icarus groped for the parachute's ripcord and hoped that Perce was right.

"Icarus? Where are you, in Zeus's name?"

Dedalus saw the gleam of something white, far ahead. It spun crazily downwards through the sky and hit the sea with a splash. Horrified, Dedalus swooped downwards. The wreckage of Icarus's wings lay floating on the sea.

"Icarus?" Dedalus circled mournfully around the wood and the feathers bobbing on the waves. "Achoo! Oh no! Icarus!"

He climbed away from the debris with a curse. "You stupid boy! I told you not to fly too close to the sun. Who am I going to get to carry out my experiments, now?"

The crazed inventor flew onwards, so busy moaning about his son's thoughtlessness that he never bothered to look up. If he had done so, he would have seen Icarus floating gently away under the canopy of his parachute.

Icarus landed in the water, released the parachute and kicked himself free. His father would be far away by now. Perce's plan had worked.

He peered into the distance and saw a small island. He would swim there and find work; perhaps become a shepherd, or keep goats. He liked animals. They didn't try to make him jump off cliffs.

Icarus would have liked to have stayed with the strangers in the future, who had been his friends for a short while. But their world wasn't his. This was where he belonged.

He began to swim towards the island and his new life.

Chapter Twelve
Floating on Air

"DO YOU RECKON Liquorice survived?" asked Well'ard.

"I don't know. That's why we're here," answered Perce as she headed towards the reference books in the school library. She had insisted on meeting

Well'ard, Eddie and Andy after school the next day.

"We could have done this at break," grumbled Well'ard.

"I was in detention at break, remember?"

"Why are you bothered about this Icarus anyway?" asked Andy, still in a bad mood after his high-diving adventures. "I'm back safe and sound. Isn't that the important thing?"

Perce just stared at him.

"She's bothered about him 'cos she fancied him," jeered Well'ard.

"Did you?" Andy gazed at her with narrowed eyes.

"No," said Perce, perhaps a little too quickly.

"What was he like?"

"Not like you at all," piped up Eddie.

"That's right," agreed Perce.

Andy beamed. Perce continued, "Not like you at all. He was intelligent, fun to be with, brave and −"

"You *did* fancy him!" Andy was shocked.

"Just kidding. Anyway, he wasn't from this world and you can't fancy a myth, can you?"

"S'pose not," grunted Andy.

Perce took the *Book of Myths* off the shelf and turned to the Legend of Icarus.

"What's it say?" inquired Eddie.

"Hang on a sec." Perce began to read. "Icarus was a ... blah, blah ... His dad was Dedalus ... blah, blah ... He made some wings ... blah, blah ... he flew too

116

close to the sun ... blah, blah ... the wax melted and he crashed into the sea and drowned."

"What a div!" exclaimed Well'ard. "We told 'im that was goin' to happen and he still went and did it! What an absolute —"

"Just a minute!" Perce was smiling. "Listen to this bit at the end: 'But some say that Icarus did not drown, but that the gods sent a small white cloud down from Olympus to bear him away to safety.'"

Well'ard looked blank.

"The parachute," explained Perce. "That was the cloud! It didn't come from Olympus, the home of the gods, it came from the airfield. He did survive!"

She was interrupted by Mr Latimer's voice outside the library door.

"Mrs Jones! Have you seen Priscilla? I've just received a message from the attendant at the swimming pool. Apparently the pool was covered in feathers again last night! If I find she had anything to do with it ..."

Perce led the others in a charge out of the back door of the library.

On the way to her house, Perce told Andy about her brilliant plan to get him back and save Icarus. She'd already told Andy all about this, but she thought he ought to hear it again anyway, just in case he'd forgotten how brilliant she'd been. Eddie and Well'ard wanted Perce to leave out the stuff about well'ard mallards, Alsatians and swans, but she didn't.

Turning into Perce's drive, they suddenly stopped dead. From the shouts and bangs that were coming from inside the house, there was obviously a major row brewing.

"Look what I've found in the dustbin! The cover from my best duvet!" Perce's mother sounded furious. "All the feathers are gone! What would your stupid daughter want with feathers?"

"She's your stupid daughter as well."

"She's in big trouble when she gets in, I can tell you."

Perce grimaced and hurried out of the drive. "Er, I reckon we won't bother going in just now. Maybe a bit later when the wrinklies have cooled down, like in a million years. Let's go somewhere else."

"We can't go to my house," growled Well'ard. "For some reason, my dad's blaming me cos he's lost his fishing net."

Eddie looked quizzical. "But you *are* to blame; you nicked it and the Alsatian ate it."

"So? That's no reason to accuse me, just cos I did it."

There was silence for a couple of minutes as they all tried to work out Well'ard's illogical logic.

"Well, how about going swimming?" suggested Eddie.

"No way!" cried Andy.

"What about the park?" asked Perce sweetly. "Oh no, sorry, boys, I forgot there's some big, hard ducks there!"

Eddie and Well'ard glared at Perce.

"I know!" Perce snapped her fingers. "Follow me."

She led the way through the streets of the town, ignoring all the boys' questions. She eventually stopped outside the amusement arcade.

"Here we go, Andy." Perce bought a token from the desk and propelled Andy through the doorway of a large white machine. "Strap up," she told him.

"Why? What is this?" hissed Andy.

Perce grinned wickedly. "It's a Flight Simulator."

Well'ard and Eddie burst out laughing.

Andy turned as white as a feather. "You must be joking."

"Don't get into a flap, you chicken. I dare you."

But Perce was talking to empty air. Andy, moving as if he had wings on his feet, flew out of the arcade, down the street and disappeared from sight.